CHANUKAH TALES
FROM OYKVETCHNIK

SCOTT HILTON DAVIS

ILLUSTRATIONS BY
AMY F. LEVINE

PUBLISHED BY
JEWISH STORYTELLER PRESS
2017

"Chaim the Chanukiyah," "Myzeleh the Mouse,"
"Reb Shimon the Shammes," and "The Pawnshop
Menorah" first appeared in *Half A Hanukkah:
Four Stories for the Festival of Lights.*

Published by
Jewish Storyteller Press
Raleigh, North Carolina, U.S.A.
www.jewishstorytellerpress.com
books@jewishstorytellerpress.com

ISBN 978-0-9975334-1-5

Library of Congress Control Number: 2017903713

For Carolyn

And know that this is but a spark
That by a miracle escaped
Of that bright light, that sacred flame,
Thy forbears kindled long ago
On altars high and pure.

—CHAIM N. BYALIK, "The Fountain," 1898
(*Translated by P. M. Raskin*)

TABLE OF CONTENTS

PREFACE

Chanukah, the Festival of Lights, has always been my favorite Jewish holiday. Since childhood, I have been drawn to the lighting of the chanukiyah (the nine-branched Chanukah menorah), the taste of my mother's freshly fried latkes, playing dreidel with my sister and friends, and the important message that encourages us to continuously fight for freedom and religious tolerance in a tumultuous world. So it's not surprising that when I finally began writing my own short stories, they turned out to be Chanukah tales set in the "Old Country"—the tiny towns and villages of Russia and Eastern Europe—before the turn of the twentieth century. For many of us who are Jewish, this was the birthplace of our *alteh bobehs* and *zaydehs*—our great-grandmothers and grandfathers.

For as long as I can remember, I have loved hearing stories about the Old Country, and over the past several years I have collected and performed them as a Jewish storyteller. Many of my favorite stories were written by four nineteenth-century Yiddish writers: Sholem Aleichem, I. L. Peretz, Sholem Abramovitsh, and Jacob Dinezon.

Although we rarely hear their names today, these four writers were once very famous and much beloved by Jewish readers all over the world. In the 1960s, Sholem Aleichem's stories about Tevye the Dairyman were turned into the Broadway musical, *Fiddler on the Roof.*

The reason these writers were so beloved was because they wrote wonderful stories about "*dos Yiddishe folk*"—the Jewish people—the teachers, tailors, blacksmiths, bakers, shopkeepers, porters, and peddlers who struggled to cope with the poverty, anti-Semitism, and violence that constantly battered their lives in the Old Country. Writing in Yiddish, the common language of more than twelve million Jews before the end of the Second World War, these writers described how people lived, loved, and struggled to remain faithful to their Jewish traditions and way of life.

Over the years, as I immersed myself in their characters, plots, and settings, a strange thing happened: I found myself writing my own Jewish stories. And lo and behold, they turned out to be Chanukah stories set in the little Old Country town of Oykvetchnik.

Oykvetchnik? Yes, Oykvetchnik—a place where people complain a lot. (Although at Chanukah time, the citizens of Oykvetchnik seem to be a little more charitable.) Similar to Sholem Aleichem's little villages of Kasrilevke and Anatevka, Oykvetchnik is filled with a variety of characters from the richest philanthropist to the lowliest beggar, all celebrating Chanukah in their own special way.

Finally, a word about the spelling of Chanukah. I've heard there are at least thirteen ways to spell the name of this holiday. Today in America, the most common spelling is "Hanukkah." The YIVO Institute for Jewish Research prefers the Yiddish transliteration, "Khanike." Since Jewish tradition allows for differing opinions, I have decided to use "Chanukah" because that's how I first learned how to spell it and because I like its "Old Country" flavor. But no matter how you spell it, I wish you a bright and joyful Festival of Lights!

Scott Hilton Davis

ONE

CHAIM THE CHANUKIYAH

Chaim the Chanukiyah was a new addition to our little synagogue in Oykvetchnik. Reb Shimon the Shammes had received him as a gift from his old friend, Reb Mendele. Reb Mendele was a book peddler who spent his whole life traveling from town to town selling holy books and sacred objects from the back of his little horse-drawn wagon.

Whenever Reb Mendele arrived in Oykvetchnik on a Friday afternoon, he would always spend *Shabbes* —the Sabbath—with Reb Shimon. They would attend shul together and then feast afterward at Reb Shimon's table. They would recite prayers, sing songs, tell stories, and argue over obscure Talmudic teachings until late into the night. And this went on until either the candles or the two old friends sputtered out—they were no spring chickens anymore, may they live to be a hundred and twenty!

One day in gratitude as Reb Mendele was heading out of town after *Shabbes,* he presented his old friend with a magnificently ornate Chanukah menorah—a chanukiyah—that unfortunately, through no fault of its own, had not sold as intended. Perhaps it was too expensive or too fancy for modern tastes.

At any rate, the fact that it happened to be a little tarnished and dusty from spending years in the back of Reb Mendele's wagon made no difference to Reb Shimon. He immediately saw the chanukiyah's dignity and beauty and accepted the gift with great appreciation.

After wishing his friend a *"Zay gezunt"*—a "Be well"—Reb Shimon carried the chanukiyah into the synagogue, gave it a good scrubbing, and buffed it so brightly it shone like the morning sun. Then he carefully placed the chanukiyah on the shelf with all the other menorahs used during the prayer services.

Chaim the Chanukiyah couldn't believe his *mazel*—his luck. Now, after so many years on the road bouncing around the back of Reb Mendele's wagon, he finally had a home—a place where he would be warm and appreciated. But as Chaim looked around at all the other menorahs, he began to feel a little out of place. All the other menorahs had seven branches, but he, Chaim the Chanukiyah, had two additional branches—nine branches in all.

And he wasn't the only one who noticed this difference. He occasionally heard some of the other menorahs whispering behind his back: "Look at that guy! He's got two extra branches. Does he really belong here with us?" And pretty soon Chaim began feeling very awkward and different.

To make matters worse, every week on *Shabbes,* Reb Shimon would take down all the other menorahs, fill them with candles, light them, and set them out in various places around the shul. But week after week, poor Chaim was left on the shelf all by himself without a single candle in his branches.

"What's wrong with me?" he wondered as he looked out at all the other menorahs filling the synagogue with their warm flickering candlelight. And Chaim felt very sad and disappointed.

One day, while Chaim was feeling especially downcast, he heard a voice call his name. "*Nu,* Chaim," said Miriam the Menorah who had just been placed beside him after services. "Why are you looking so forlorn?"

"*Oy*, Miriam, I don't understand it," replied Chaim with sadness in his voice. "Reb Shimon never takes me off the shelf. Yet you and all the other menorahs get candles every *Shabbes*."

"And you're complaining?" interrupted Motl the Menorah who was standing beside Miriam. "At least you get to rest on *Shabbes*. The rest of us have to work!"

"Sha, Motl," said Miriam. "It's not working, it's holy service! And your time to serve will come too, Chaim. Just be patient."

"It will?" asked Chaim.

"Of course, it will," replied Miriam. "You're a very special menorah, and Reb Shimon is saving you for a very special holiday."

"He is? What sort of holiday is it?"

"*Oy!*" exclaimed Motl. "Don't you know about Chanukah?"

"Chanukah?" asked Chaim.

"*Vey iz mir,*" grumbled Motl, "what a *schlemiel!*"

"Motl, be nice!" said Miriam. "Listen, Chaim, just wait a little longer. I promise that Dovidl the Dreidel will explain everything to you when the time is right."

"Dovidl the Dreidel," thought Chaim. "I can't wait to meet him."

But it was so hard for Chaim to be patient. As the days passed, dust began to float down and settle on him.

His shine began to fade. And then a spider spun an intricate web around his branches and made a little home in one of his candleholders. As the weeks passed, Chaim became more and more dejected. Until the arrival of the month of Kislev.

Suddenly, just as Miriam predicted, Reb Shimon the Shammes came up to Chaim and took him off the shelf. He wiped the dust from his branches, gave him a good polishing, placed him on a table in the center of the synagogue, and filled all his branches with candles.

Then Reb Shimon reached into his pocket and pulled out a very strange looking object. It was made of lead and had a point on one end and a short little handle on the other. It had four sides, and on each side was inscribed a Hebrew letter. Reb Shimon set the object on the table and walked away.

To Chaim's surprise, the strange looking object started talking to him in a gruff little voice: "*Nu*, you must be the new kid in town."

"Are you talking to me?" asked Chaim. "Do I know you?"

"Not yet. But I already got an earful about you from the Menorahs—Miriam and Motl. I'm Dovidl the Dreidel."

"Dovidl the Dreidel!" exclaimed Chaim. "I've been waiting to meet you for so long! Miriam said you would explain Chanukah to me."

"*Oy vey,*" muttered Dovidl. "A chanukiyah who doesn't know the story of Chanukah?"

"You'll forgive me," said Chaim. "I've spent most of my life in the back of Reb Mendele's wagon. He hardly ever said a word to me. I think I disappointed him."

"All right, kid," said Dovidl softening. "This is your lucky day. It will be my pleasure to fill you in on all the details." Whereupon Dovidl the Dreidel lifted himself up onto his point and slowly began to spin the tale of Chanukah for his new friend.

"It all began when the evil King Antiochus invaded Judea, desecrated the Holy Temple in Jerusalem, and ordered his soldiers to convert all the Jews to the Greek religion upon pain of death. But a priest named Mattathias rebelled and with his five sons escaped to the mountains where they gathered together a band of fighters called 'The Maccabees.'

"Mattathias's son Judah became their leader, and he led his men into combat against Antiochus's vast army—an army that had more soldiers, better weapons, and even elephants to lead the charge! A terrible battle was fought, and when it was all over, Antiochus's army was defeated!"

"Praise God!" exclaimed Chaim.

"Indeed!" replied Dovidl. "From the battlefield, Judah marched his fighters to Jerusalem where they took back the Holy Temple and re-sanctified it. Then Judah Maccabee proclaimed an eight-day festival, and commanded that all the sacred menorahs be filled with holy oil and set ablaze. But the synagogue attendants could only find enough purified oil to last for one day."

"*Oy,* what happened, Dovidl?" gasped Chaim.

"What happened? When they lit the great menorahs, the sacred oil burned for eight days and eight nights, shining a holy light over the land of Judea.

"A miracle!" declared Chaim.

"Yes," agreed Dovidl. "And that's what my Hebrew letters stand for: *Nun, gimel, hay, shin*—'*Nes gadol hayah sham*'—'A great miracle happened there!' And that's why you have eight branches, Chaim, to always remember and celebrate the eight days of Chanukah."

"But Dovidl, I have nine branches," said Chaim.

"Yes, of course you do," replied Dovidl. "Your *middle* branch is for the shammes candle—the helper candle—used to light all the other candles while the Chanukah blessings are recited each evening."

Suddenly, it all made sense to Chaim: that as a chanukiyah, his special role was to hold the candles during the holiday of Chanukah.

And there, on the final night of Chanukah, as the whole congregation gathered together, and as Miriam, Motl, and all the other menorahs looked down from their shelf, Chaim stood with great dignity in the center of the little shul, his polished branches all aglow with flaming candles. And as he saw his reflection in the windowpane, he finally understood that as a chanukiyah, he was a beacon of religious freedom to the whole world—a freedom won all those years ago by the brave and courageous Maccabees.

And as Chaim stood there radiant and proud, he knew for certain that he finally had a home in Oykvetchnik.

Two

Myzeleh the Mouse

"Myzeleh" was the name most people called him on those rare occasions when they spotted him in the yeshiva—the Oykvetchnik academy of Jewish learning. "Myzeleh," the Yiddish word for "little mouse."

The yeshiva was a quiet little place, where people prayed, studied Torah, Talmud, the Holy Scriptures, and even a little Kabbalah once in awhile. For poor old men and unfortunate young boys with no one to support them and nowhere else to live, the yeshiva was also a place of shelter for the night—and sometimes even longer.

Myzeleh had made his home in the basement of the yeshiva behind a box of broken menorahs and dented *Shabbes* candlesticks. As a matter of principle, he tried very hard to mind his own business. He stayed out of people's way, and for the most part, no one paid him much attention. Even Khatskl the Cat who showed up every now and then to prowl around hardly ever noticed him. Perhaps Khatskl knew that having a mouse or two around the yeshiva was good for job security.

Now, Myzeleh had a gift: he was a very good listener and from time to time, one of the young boys from the yeshiva would come downstairs to talk. Of course, that wasn't their initial purpose for coming to visit. Usually, they didn't even know that Myzeleh was there. Mostly they just made their way down to the basement to escape—to escape from the rigors of studying, the pangs of hunger, or the pains of loneliness. And what could Myzeleh do? He understood all these things himself—except maybe not the studying—but he knew that life was not easy for the boys upstairs in the yeshiva.

So if someone came down to visit, and he thought it was safe, he would peek out from around the corner of the box of broken menorahs and dented *Shabbes* candlesticks. And if Khatskl wasn't around and the coast was clear, he would scurry to a stack of discarded prayer books, jump on top, and assume a thoughtful pose. He figured it was a mitzvah—a good deed—to just listen. And this is how Myzeleh the Mouse met Borekh the Orphan.

Myzeleh, like everyone else in the yeshiva, knew Borekh had no parents or relatives. His mother had died in childbirth, and when his father died a short time later, poor thing, he was brought to the yeshiva with little more than the clothes on his back. His only possession was a rusty little pocketknife from his father, which he treasured like life itself.

Reb Yosele, the good-hearted caretaker of the yeshiva, took pity on the poor boy and gave him a little food and a bench to sleep on.

And over time, Borekh became Reb Yosele's assistant, cleaning up, bringing in water, chopping firewood, running errands, and going for this and that. And in the few spare minutes he had for himself, Borekh would sit on his bench and use his little pocketknife to whittle on sticks he brought in from the woodpile.

"What are you carving?" the other boys asked him. And Borekh always replied, "Nothing."

And it was true. For nothing ever seemed to appear from the little stick that grew thinner and thinner as the little pile of shavings grew taller and taller at his feet.

One time, Reb Hershele the Water Carrier sat down beside Borekh and asked, "What are you carving?"

"Nothing," replied Borekh.

"I see," said Reb Hershele in a kindly voice. "Here, Borekh, let me show you something."

Reaching into his pocket, Reb Hershele pulled out a pearl-handled pocketknife, sleek and shiny. From another pocket, he pulled out a small block of wood. As Borekh watched in amazement, Reb Hershele's knife cut and chipped and chiseled away until the head of a little dog emerged from the wood.

"Hear me, Borekh," Reb Hershele said, "if you can see it in your mind, your knife will find it in the wood."

But as hard as Borekh tried, he could never find anything in the sticks of wood he whittled on for hours and hours with his rusty little pocketknife.

One day, in deep sadness and frustration, Borekh wandered down to the basement of the yeshiva. "Why can't I carve anything?" he grumbled to himself as he stared at the stick in his hand. Looking up in disgust, he found Myzeleh staring back at him from atop a stack of old prayer books.

At first, Borekh was startled and raised the stick to throw it. But then he thought, "Why should I hurt the little mouse? What has he done to me?" And it didn't take long before Borekh was pouring out his heart to Myzeleh.

What did Myzeleh do? *Nu,* what could he do? He listened. And over the next few weeks, Borekh came back several times to whittle and talk and ask the question, "What shall I carve?"

Sometimes Borekh would bring little bits of apple, tiny chunks of cheese, a few nuts, and on very rare occasions, a sweet of some sort, which he always shared with Myzeleh. Then he would sit and whittle and talk. And what did he talk about? He talked about his parents and how he missed them, and how he wished that they would come to him in a dream so he could get to know them better.

He talked about Reb Yosele and how grateful he was to be his assistant. He talked about learning how to carve like Reb Hershele the Water Carrier so he could make little animals for all the boys in the yeshiva. But mostly he talked about his great longing to be a *mentsh* —a real person—with a real job and a real home, and who knows, maybe even a real wife and children someday.

But Borekh always ended with the same question: "What shall I carve, Myzeleh?" And Myzeleh felt bad because he never had an answer for him.

One evening, when Myzeleh heard footsteps on the stairs, he came running out to greet Borekh. But *oy vey,* to his surprise he came face-to-face with Katskl the Cat on the prowl for food. When Katskl saw Myzeleh, he pounced, barely missing the little mouse.

Scurrying away, Myzeleh leaped into the box of bent menorahs and dented *Shabbes* candlesticks and hid himself beneath the heavy brass objects. Katskl sniffed around the box and then began to climb inside—

"What are you doing down there!" a voice called out from the top of the stairs. It was Borekh, just in time!

"Get out of here, Cat! Get out of here now!" shouted Borekh and Katskl dashed out of the basement.

In great relief, Myzeleh slowly climbed up from the bottom of the box. That's when he spotted it: the answer to Borekh's question, "What shall I carve?"

"Myzeleh, are you all right?" asked Borekh.

Myzeleh peeked over the edge of the box of broken menorahs and dented *Shabbes* candlesticks to be sure that Katskl was really gone.

"I was worried about you," said Borekh.

Myzeleh hurried to the stack of discarded prayer books as Borekh sat down with his rusty pocketknife in one hand and a stick of wood in the other.

"Remember what Reb Hershele told you," Borekh muttered to himself. "'If you can see it in your mind, the knife will find it in the wood,' But what? What shall I carve?"

"I know what you should carve," thought Myzeleh. "And it's perfect for Chanukah! But how am I going to tell you?"

As Borekh aimlessly chipped away at the stick in his hand, Myzeleh suddenly got an idea. He leaped off the prayer books and jumped onto the box filled with broken menorahs and dented *Shabbes* candlesticks. Making sure he had Borekh's attention, he danced around the objects, then dove down into the box and came back up again. Jumping to the floor, he scampered around the box, leaped back onto one of the broken menorahs, and danced a little hora.

Borekh watched in disbelief. "Myzeleh, what are you doing?"

Again Myzeleh dove down into the box, then leaped up and jumped from the branch of a broken menorah to a dented *Shabbes* candlestick. He vaulted down to the floor, ran to Borekh, circled his feet, sprang up to his knee, onto his shoulder, up to his head, then jumped down to the bench and returned to the box of broken menorahs and dented *Shabbes* candlesticks.

"What is it, you *meshugeneh* mouse? You're acting crazy!"

"*Oy*," thought Myzeleh as he tried to catch his breath. "I've got to do it again!"

So off he went, leaping from one broken menorah to another. He circled around a *Shabbes* candlestick and dove down into the box before coming back up for a little dance.

Slowly Borekh got up and walked over to the box. "Myzeleh, are you trying to tell me something?"

"Yes," Myzeleh thought. "Yes!" Quickly he scampered over to the stack of discarded prayer books as Borekh began removing tarnished brass objects from the box: menorahs with broken branches, dented *Shabbes* candlesticks, crumpled Kiddush cups and spice boxes, the spigot from an old brass samovar, and at the very bottom, what Myzeleh had so wanted him to find: a small brass dreidel.

As Borekh lifted it up to take a closer look, he could see why it had been discarded. The handle was twisted and bent, making the dreidel impossible to spin. But the dreidel's form was right there before his eyes.

"A dreidel!" exclaimed Borekh. "Myzeleh, maybe I could carve a wooden dreidel!"

And as Myzeleh looked on, Borekh sat down and began to cut and chip and chisel away at his piece of wood. First he made a block, then he cut the point, then one-by-one he carved the Hebrew letters, *Nun, Gimel, Hay, Shin* for "*Nes gadol hayah sham*"—"A great miracle happened there."

Finally, ever so carefully, Borekh carved the little handle. And wouldn't you know it, after all those hours of whittling sticks, the handle turned out as true, straight, and smooth as an arrow. When he was done, he gave the dreidel a spin, and it worked perfectly.

"I did it, Myzeleh!" said Borekh.

"Yes," Myzeleh thought, "and I am so proud of you, my friend. You have become a real *mentsh!*"

* * * * *

Several days passed before Borekh returned to the basement. Chanukah was almost over, and Myzeleh had begun to worry.

"Myzeleh, are you down here?"

When Myzeleh heard Borekh's voice, he scampered out to greet him. But Borekh looked different somehow, taller and more confident, but also a little sad. In his hand, he held a little bag.

"Here, Myzeleh," said Borekh, "I've brought you something to *nosh* on," and he placed a handful of nuts and cheese in a little pile on the floor.

"Myzeleh, I've come to tell you something. I'm leaving the yeshiva. I've come to say goodbye."

"Goodbye?" Myzeleh couldn't believe his ears. His tail drooped and his eyes filled with tears.

"Myzeleh, don't be sad. It's a good thing, really. Reb Tsalik the Furniture Maker saw my dreidel, and he offered me a job on the spot! He promised to teach me everything he knows about woodcarving!

"And don't worry, Myzeleh, I'll come back to visit. Truly, I will! And look, I brought you a little gift—a Chanukah present—something I carved with my own hands!"

Opening the bag, Borekh pulled out a little wooden house with a little wooden roof, a little wooden window, and a little wooden door with a little wooden lock. There was even a little wooden mezuzah on the doorpost.

Borekh set the little house behind the box of broken menorahs and dented *Shabbes* candlesticks and stepped back so as not to frighten Myzeleh.

"Here, Myzeleh, try it out," said Borekh. "This should keep you safe from that old cat upstairs!"

"Could this be a trap?" Myzeleh wondered? "Was it really safe to go inside?"

But then he thought, "Imagine, actually living in my own home!" So very carefully Myzeleh entered the little wooden house—not forgetting to kiss the mezuzah on the way in. It was very spacious, and he could see Borekh smiling at him through the little wooden window.

"You be a good mouse, Myzeleh. Stay out of trouble. I'll miss you very much."

Then Borekh headed upstairs and left the yeshiva to become a woodcarver.

"*Zay gezunt,* Borekh," thought Myzeleh. "Be well, my friend, and go in good health."

THREE

DVORAH ROHKL'S
CHANUKAH PARTY

Dvorah Rohkl Rabinovitz was a pillar of Oykvetch-nik society. Her husband, Reb Avrom, was the town's richest man, a successful merchant, and an important official in the synagogue, where, of course, he had a prominent seat near the Eastern Wall.

He was also, at Dvorah Rohkl's insistence, Oy-kvetchnik's most reliable and generous philanthropist, giving dutifully, if perhaps not so enthusiastically, to every charity and good cause that touched his wife's kind heart. Which, it must be said, was easily moved by a tear-filled story, a worthy community endeavor, or a persistent beggar.

This is why Reb Avrom was doing everything in his power to keep Reb Sholem, the headmaster of the Talmud Torah—the community school for poor children—away from his wife.

You see, Reb Sholem had made it known after morning services that he was gathering funds for a small Chanukah party to permit his young students to properly celebrate the Festival of Lights. Upon hearing this, Reb Avrom immediately contributed a few rubles, knowing full well that if his mitzvah-minded wife got wind of Reb Sholem's request, he, Reb Avrom, would be shelling out a much bigger donation.

Reb Avron could already hear his beloved Dvorah Rokhl: "Husband, this is such an important cause, teaching our young people about the victory of the Maccabees, the preservation of our religious freedom, and the miracle of the holy oil that lasted for eight days. We must help them celebrate this holiday!"

So by making an early contribution, Reb Avrom hoped to prevent Reb Sholem from making a direct appeal to his wife, and as a way of furthering this aim, he hurried home to bar the door in case the good headmaster tried to visit Dvorah Rokhl. But when he arrived home, his wife was gone.

"Where is she?" demanded Reb Avrom of the servant, and was told Dvorah Rokhl had gone to the marketplace with the cook to buy food for *Shabbes*.

Reb Avrom's heart sank. His wife was sure to run into Reb Sholem at the marketplace, and if that happened, his contribution to the Chanukah party was guaranteed to increase significantly.

An hour later, Dvorah Rokhl and the cook returned with baskets full of food. And sure enough, Reb Avrom's worst fear was realized: Reb Sholem the Talmud Torah headmaster was right behind them.

"Dear husband," said Dvorah Rokhl, "you must hear the wonderful plan Reb Sholem has to celebrate Chanukah with his students."

"*Oy gevalt,*" thought Reb Avrom, "how much is this going to cost me?" But all he said was, "Yes, my dear, of course."

And just as Reb Avrom had expected, Dvorah Rokhl's enthusiasm for Reb Sholem's idea was unbounded. "How wonderful," she exclaimed, "a Chanukah party for the boys! And why only for the boys? Why not invite the girls, too? And what about their parents? Shouldn't they be included? And if the parents are coming, how can we leave out the grandparents? In fact, while we're at it, why don't we just invite the whole town of Oykvetchnik!"

"The whole town?" asked Reb Avrom, trying not to clutch at his heart.

"Why not?" replied Dvorah Rokhl. "Dear husband, make a contribution! They will need more menorahs and candles; they will need potatoes, eggs, and oil for latkes; and a klezmer band for music!"

That was all it took. By the time Reb Sholem headed back to the Talmud Torah, he had all the money he needed for the whole town of Oykvetchnik to celebrate Chanukah. And, of course, it was all coming out of Reb Avrom's pocket.

Now in defense of Reb Avrom, may no shame befall him, he was not a hard-hearted man. Nor was he unwilling to contribute his fair share. On the contrary, Reb Avrom praised God for his success and was fully aware that he had an obligation to give charity. But his idea of a sufficient contribution always conflicted with his wife's. If he said one, she said ten. If he said ten, she said one hundred. And as he handed out ruble after ruble, Reb Avrom always became more and more depressed.

"What's wrong?" Dvorah Rokhl would ask him. But what could he say? "You're depleting our bank account, our retirement nest egg, our children's inheritance?"

And to make matters worse, since everyone considered his wife a *guteh neshomeh*—a good soul—people came from far and wide to seek her advice, cry on her shoulder, and ask for her help. And whenever she asked Reb Avrom to give, she would always remind him, "*Tzedakah* is a mitzvah, good husband, a good deed and a commandment!" And how could he argue with her? So he fell deeper and deeper into a dark despair.

Which is exactly how Reb Avrom was feeling as he watched the whole town of Oykvetchnik celebrate Chanukah at the Talmud Torah. Candles burned in numerous menorahs around the large room. A klezmer band was playing festive music and platters of latkes were being served to people who ate them like there was no tomorrow.

"Dear husband," said Dvorah Rokhl as she sat down beside him. "Have you ever seen such a joyous Chanukah celebration?"

"*Oy,*" he thought, "if she only knew how much this 'joyous celebration' was costing us." But he just nodded.

Dvorah Rokhl smiled and pointed across the room. There on the floor, Reb Avrom saw his grandchildren laughing and clapping in delight as they spun their little dreidels.

Suddenly, a memory flickered before Reb Avrom's eyes: a Chanukah when there was no celebration, no candles, no latkes, no dreidels. The terrible year when his father died, and his mother barely had enough money to put food on the table.

He was just a boy, and the years that followed were hard and painful, until at last he was old enough to work and help support the family. And by his own labor and luck—one miserable menial job at a time—he earned enough money to start his own business, a business that, praise God, prospered beyond his wildest dreams.

The klezmer music suddenly grew louder and faster, and as people began to twirl and dance, flying past Reb Avrom with grateful smiles on their faces, he recalled the Chanukah parties Dvorah Rokhl insisted they have each year for their own children—celebrations that filled up the house with so much light and warmth and love.

And Reb Avrom realized that in the same way that God provided an abundance of oil for the Jews of Judea that lasted for eight days and eight nights, the Holy One would provide him with all he needed to support his wife and children.

And there they all were, his beloved wife by his side, and his children and grandchildren celebrating with everyone else in the town!

Before you know it, his toe began to tap, his body began to sway, and almost imperceptibly a smile appeared on his lips, hidden deep within his full bushy gray beard.

Only Dvorah Rohkl saw it, and she gently touched his hand. "Happy Chanukah, dear husband," she whispered.

"Yes, dear wife," replied Reb Avrom. "Happy Chanukah to everyone in Oykvetchnik."

FOUR

HOW OYKVETCHNIK
GOT ITS NAME

People are always asking me why Chanukah is so important in Oykvetchnik. "Is Chanukah," they ask me, "as important as Passover, or Purim, or Rosh Hashanah, or Yom Kippur?" Heaven forbid we should compare them all in the same breath!

Well, I'll tell you, it all began with the arrival of a poor candle peddler nearly half a century ago. A candle peddler named Nochum Kvetchner who found himself trudging along the route between Warsaw, the capital of Poland, and Vilna, the capital of Lithuania.

On a cold day in the month of Kislev, halfway between these two great cities, which just happen to be exactly two hundred and fifty miles apart, Nochum the Candle Peddler arrived at a deserted crossroads. Tired and weary, he dropped his heavy pack on the ground, sat down with a groan, and collapsed in defeat.

Nochum was a short man with a full red beard and a ruddy, sunburned face. His long black coat was covered with mud and dust, and beneath his battered and frayed peddler's cap, his once hopeful eyes were dark and discouraged.

"*Oy,*" he moaned, "my aching back, my aching feet, my aching bones!" And then he wept, this poor *schlimazel* whose luck had never been good, sobbing in despair as he inquired of the Eternal One why fortune had so completely abandoned him.

There's an old Yiddish expression: "If a Jew sells candles, the sun will never go down." And this was Nochum's *mazel*—his luck. Which didn't make any sense, because selling candles seemed like a sure thing.

"Don't Jews need candles?" asked the *gonif*—the thief—who talked Nochum into buying his candle peddling business.

"Jews need candles in their homes, in their synagogues, even in their little study houses. Candles, lots of candles! Candles for *Shabbes* and the holidays, candles for Havdalah, *yorzeit* candles to remember their departed ones, and, of course, candles for Chanukah—every year, lots and lots of Chanukah candles!"

So Nochum Kvetchner bought the candle peddler's business. But in the year he had trudged between Warsaw and Vilna, even as the sun set precisely on schedule, Jews, may no evil befall them, completely stopped buying candles!

Now it's true, times were very hard and people very poor. People struggled to put food on the table and keep a roof over their heads. As hard as Nochum Kvetchner the candle peddler tried, he could barely eke out a living.

Which is why he sat there on the ground at the crossroads a broken man in complete desolation. Chanukah was just around the corner, his peddler's pack was filled to overflowing with Chanukah candles, and all his hopes and ambitions had melted away like yesterday's snow.

When out of the blue, at the very moment when everything seemed lost, along came Malkeh Hennoch the Egg Seller. She was riding in a little cart being pulled along by a little horse, and behind her were stacks of baskets filled with fresh eggs—brown, white, and speckled.

Malkeh Hennoch was a stout and sturdy young woman. She was eighteen years old and had a sweet round face with cheeks made rosy from hours in the sun. She wore a colored kerchief on her head and a clean white apron over her faded pink dress.

Her only little quirk—if you could call it that—was a tendency to say "*Oy!*" whenever she worried about something. And with her kind heart, she seemed to worry about everything! In fact, she said "*Oy*" so often people began calling her "*Oy* Malkeh."

Oy Malkeh's parents owned a little farm near the crossroads, and Malkeh's job was to care for the chickens. As she often told her friends, "I feed the chickens, and the chickens feed us."

When Malkeh spotted Nochum on the ground, she stopped her little cart. "*Oy,*" she said, "are you injured?"

"*Oy,*" replied Nochum. "Worse than injured. I'm dying!"

"*Oy gevalt,*" gasped Malkeh. "Dying?"

"Yes, dying! Look at me. A peddler who can't sell his merchandise is as good as dead."

"*Oy,*" said Malkeh. "What kind of merchandise are you selling?"

"Candles."

"Candles?"

"Yes, candles! Candles for *Shabbes* and the holidays, candles for Havdalah, *yorzeit* candles, and general everyday run-of-the-mill candles."

"What about Chanukah candles?" she asked.

"Do I have Chanukah candles? What, do you think I'm such a *schlemiel* I don't know this is Chanukah time? Of course, I have candles for Chanukah. I've got candles for Chanukah coming out of my ears!

"Do you have any idea how many candles you need for Chanukah? When you're counting out candles for Chanukah, you don't just start with one candle on the first day; you start with two because you always have to include the shammes candle, right?

"So on the first day you have two candles, and on the second day, you have three candles. On the third day you have four candles, on the fourth day five candles, and on the fifth day, you have six candles.

"Day six comes along, you need seven candles; day seven, eight candles; and on the final day of Chanukah, you have eight candles plus the shammes candle which makes nine candles. So when you add it all up, you know how many candles you need?"

"Seventy-two," said Malkeh.

"How do you know that?" asked Nochum.

"I counted it up in my head," replied Malkeh.

"*Nu*, that's a very smart head!" admitted Nochum. "Perhaps you also know in Kabbalah seventy-two is a very auspicious number!"

"*Oy*," said Malkeh.

"*Oy*, is right," agreed Nochum.

"No," replied Malkeh. "*Oy*, this is a miracle."

"A miracle?" asked Nochum.

"Yes, a miracle! *Oy,* a terrible tragedy has befallen us. Libe-Zissel, who owned the candle stall in the market-place since time began, left us for the World to Come, may she rest in peace. People are desperate for candles —especially Chanukah candles. How can you properly celebrate Chanukah without candles? *Oy,* we were all afraid the holiday was ruined."

"*Oy,*" said Nochum jumping to his feet. "This is a sign from heaven! Please, dear lady, show me to the marketplace!" and he lifted his pack onto his back with an "*Oy!*"

"*Oy,*" said Malkeh, "I'll do better than that. Climb into the cart and I'll take you there."

And there in the marketplace, it *was* like a miracle! When people heard Nochum Kvetchner had candles, they came running as if he had brought merchandise from the Promised Land. Kopecks flew at him from all directions as he emptied his entire peddler's bag. By the end of the day, every single candle was sold!

And Malkeh, who had been selling her eggs right beside him, had the same good fortune. Every basket was empty; every egg was gone!

"*Oy,*" said Malkeh.

"*Oy,*" agreed Nochum.

And if it had been permitted, they would've hugged each other right there on the spot. Instead, they just smiled at each other with great pleasure.

That evening, Malkeh took Nochum home to meet her parents. After a good supper, Nochum was invited to spend the night—in the barn.

The next morning, Nochum, his spirits renewed, made a proposal to Malkeh's parents—not a marriage proposal; that would come later through a matchmaker and result in a very happy marriage with many children. Ahh, but that's another story.

Anyhow, Nochum, the consummate salesman, had come up with a vision for a new business. Since so many Jews were now traveling back and forth between the great cities of Vilna and Warsaw—hungry Jews in need of a kosher meal—why not set up a little stand at the crossroads to serve hardboiled eggs and bagels?

Everyone agreed this was a brilliant idea, and so, as they say in the egg business, a plan was hatched, and to everyone's delight, the new business not only flourished, it became a great success! Soon the little stand turned into a little restaurant, the restaurant into a little inn, and the inn into a little hotel.

Pretty soon a blacksmith arrived and set up a little shop with a horse stable in the back. Then a little general store was established, and as it prospered, vendors from the marketplace began opening up little shops around it.

Of course, how can a Jewish community exist without a synagogue? So as more and more people moved in, a committee was formed and a rabbi was found to start a little shul.

Before you know it, the little crossroads—halfway between Warsaw, the capital of Poland, and Vilna, the capital of Lithuania—turned into a little town.

Naturally, a town needs a name, and as people began asking each other, "What should we call ourselves?" someone remembered the day all those years ago when *Oy* Malkeh the Egg Seller rescued Reb Kvetchner the Candle Peddler and saved Chanukah. That was the day when luck arrived at the crossroads. It was a real miracle!

And so all the citizens made a unanimous decision —which was another miracle at the crossroads! They combined the names of *Oy* Malkeh and Reb Kvetchner to create the town of Oykvetchnik!

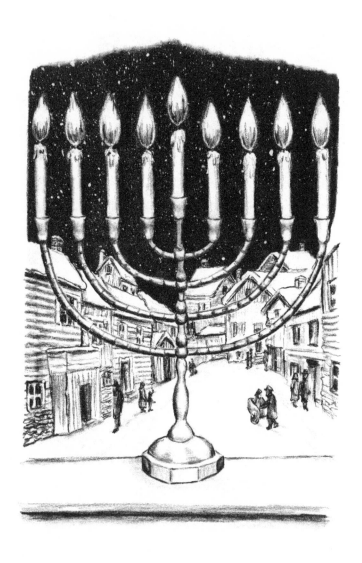

FIVE

REB SHIMON THE SHAMMES

Reb Shimon the Shammes was the caretaker of the synagogue in our tiny shtetl town of Oykvetchnik. He would arise early—often before sunrise—and head out into the community, banging on shutters to summon Jews to morning prayers.

Late at night, after the final scholar had sleepily stumbled out of the little shul, he would replace the holy books on their shelves, sweep up the floors, and snuff out any remaining candles.

On those rare occasions when some poor stranger had no place else to stay, Reb Shimon would take him home and feed him from his own table. Then off to bed he would go, only to start the whole routine all over again the next morning.

And Reb Shimon had been doing this for as long as anyone could remember, including Reb Shimon himself. In fact, that was the problem plaguing Reb Shimon at this very moment: Remembering. He was finding it harder and harder to remember things.

"Don't worry about it," said his old friend, Reb Meshulem, as they *noshed* on a bagel one morning after services. "It happens to all of us. It's called getting old."

"But it *does* worry me," admitted Reb Shimon. "What if I forget something important? Like forgetting to wash my hands before a meal? Or, God forbid, forgetting to say the blessing after bodily functions?"

"So long as you don't forget the bodily functions!" replied Reb Meshulem with a little chuckle. "*Nu,* Reb Shimon, maybe it's time to start thinking about retiring."

"Retiring? I'm not ready for that!" grumbled Reb Shimon as he left the table in a huff.

But all day long, as Reb Shimon went about his duties, the idea of retiring kept creeping into his thoughts. Not because he didn't feel strong and capable, but because he was struggling with his memory. Forgetting someone's name or where you laid your glasses was one thing, but it was now the day before Chanukah, and

Reb Shimon could not—for the life of him—remember where he put the menorah.

He had already bought the candles from Chavele the Candlemaker and a brand new box of matches. Yet when he went looking for the big menorah in the synagogue, he couldn't find it. He looked everywhere, high and low, in every nook and cranny. He looked in the closet where he kept the Kiddush cup, the spice box, and the *Shabbes* candlesticks.

He looked in the cabinet where he kept the Seder trays. He checked behind the Torah in the Ark and even peeked into the Rabbi's study. Nothing! He couldn't find it anywhere.

"*Oy*, Master of the Universe," he pleaded, "what am I going to do?"

He didn't have enough money to buy a new one, and who would believe he simply misplaced such a large and holy object? And God forbid, what if people accused him of stealing it!

Oy, what was he to do? If ever there was a time for a Chanukah miracle, this was it. And so, of course, as in all good Jewish stories, a miracle arrived.

That evening, to everyone's surprise, into the synagogue came a rich and fancy gentleman. He had a trimmed beard, the latest hat, and his clothes were tailored like a prince.

He walked up to Reb Shimon and said, "Reb Shimon, I thought you would've come to see me by now."

Reb Shimon just stared. The man looked vaguely familiar, but Reb Shimon couldn't place him.

"Don't you recognize me, Reb Shimon?" the man asked.

"You'll forgive me, I can't pull up your name right now."

"It's me, Reb Shimon, Moishe Pechenik, and I've come to repay your mitzvah—your good deed!"

"My mitzvah?"

"Yes! You don't remember, Reb Shimon?"

"*Nu*, please, refresh my memory."

"*Oy*," the man began, "last winter, shortly after Chanukah, I came to see you in great despair. I had lost my job as a lumber merchant, and my wife was deathly ill. She needed a special doctor, but I couldn't afford to pay him.

"You were carrying the big menorah, and you handed it to me, just like that. You said, 'Here, take this. We won't need it again until next year. Pawn it and get yourself a little money. Reb Yankel the Pawnbroker will take good care of it. But don't forget, we need it back next year for Chanukah.

"So I did what you told me, Reb Shimon. I pawned the menorah, and with the money, I paid the doctor. And praise God, my wife recovered.

"But listen to this Reb Shimon: the doctor told me his brother had just married into a wealthy family that owned a large estate filled with forests full of trees. They were starting a lumber company and they needed some-one to manage the business.

"'I'm a lumber merchant,' I told him, and because I had paid his bill so promptly, he put me in touch with his brother.

"Well, to make a long story short, your mitzvah not only helped heal my wife—long life to her—it led me to a new job, a wonderful career, and—no evil eye— a very good livelihood if I do say so myself. And all because of your good deed, Reb Shimon!"

"Praise God," said Reb Shimon, delighted with the man's good fortune. "But tell me this, Reb Moishe, do you have the menorah?"

"Of course, I have the menorah—and a whole lot more! And I will deliver it all tomorrow night for Chan-ukah."

And sure enough, Reb Moishe Pechenik was true to his word. He arrived with the menorah polished more brightly than anyone had ever seen it before. And along with him came servants carrying platters of latkes, bowls of sour cream, and bottles of brandy. And after the bless-ings and the lighting of the menorah, everyone sat down to eat in joyful celebration.

And as Reb Shimon stared at the beautiful menorah standing there all aglow on the synagogue's windowsill, he vowed to himself that no matter how bad his memory got, he would never forget this Chanukah night.

Six

Peter Markovich
the Soldier

Many still remember the great sadness that fell upon the town of Oykvetchnik on that terrible day when the military officials came for the boys who had been drafted into Tsar Nikolai's army. The memory still haunts those who watched the frightened young men being marched down the road and out of sight.

Only one walked with his shoulders back and his head held high. His name was Pinchas ben Mordechai. He was eighteen years old, sturdy as an ox, and the fourth son of a simple tailor.

The night before, Pinchas's father had taken him aside. "Be strong, my son," he said. "They may cut your beard. They may force you to eat forbidden foods. But you must always remain a Jew.

"If they knock you down, get up. If they spit on you, wipe it off. If they fight with you, fight back. They may beat you, but they will see you are no coward.

"Always remember the Maccabees, my son. They were great warriors. Remember the strength of Mattathias who slew the traitor, remember the courage of Judah who was victorious in battle, and always remember the power of the Holy One who defeated Antiochus and his army. Remain a Jew, my son, and, God willing, you will be protected on your long journey."

And so the next morning, Pinchas ben Mordechai marched off to meet his fate in the Tsar's army. A journey that would last for twenty-five years—if he survived.

His father was right. On his very first day as a soldier, they cut his hair, his sidelocks, and his beard. That afternoon they changed his name from Pinchas ben Mordechai to Peter Markovich. For dinner, they served him a stew filled with pork. He nearly choked on it.

He was taught how to march, how to shoot a rifle, how to bayonet the enemy. He fought against the Turks in the Caucasus and the revolutionaries of the Polish Rebellion. He was always on the front lines because Jews were always ordered to the front lines by their Russian commanders.

And day-by-day, march-by-march, battle-by-battle, Peter Markovich found himself drifting further and further away from his Jewish life in Oykvetchnik. He endured the thunder of cannons, the advancing barrage of rifle fire, and the screams of wounded soldiers. Yet somehow he made it through.

Then, only a few months before his enlistment was over, he was sent to guard the frontiers of Siberia. There, in that frozen wasteland, a new commander ordered him to stand guard—to stand guard on one of the coldest nights of the year!

He was cold. So cold he was sure this would be his last guard duty. The freezing wind blurred his vision and numbed his senses. In the morning they were certain to find him crumpled in the snow or standing upright like a frozen statue.

As the darkness deepened, he was ordered to put out the small campfire. "Snipers," was the commander's excuse as he headed back to the warm barracks, although a sniper's bullet might have been more merciful than freezing to death.

The wind howled, and the snow grew deeper and thicker. Peter Markovich stomped his feet and beat his gloved hands against his chest. He tugged at his cap, pulled the earflaps down, and raised up his muffler to cover his face.

That's when he saw the flickering light in the distance. Fear surged through his body. Was this the enemy —a glimpse of a sniper through the trees?

He raised his rifle to his shoulder. "Halt! Who goes there?" he shouted, but no one answered. All he heard was the wind, the cold, freezing wind. All he saw was the white swirling snow.

Slowly, very slowly, he moved towards the light. As the light grew brighter and brighter, he tightened his finger on the trigger, ready to fire.

Suddenly, he stopped dead in his tracks. Before him stood a small, rickety old hut made of logs and wooden shingles. The flickering light was coming through the window: nine candles burning in a Chanukah menorah.

How had he missed seeing it before? How had he missed seeing these flickering candles?

He tried peeking in the window but couldn't see anyone. Cautiously, rifle raised, he approached the door and knocked, then knocked again more forcefully. Slowly, the door opened, and an old man stood before him looking frail and frightened. He had a full gray beard parted in the middle; his skin was pale, but his eyes were black as coal. He wore a heavy coat, and his head was covered with a yarmulke.

"*Sholem aleichem,*" Peter Markovich said lowering his rifle. "Peace unto you."

The old man gasped. "*Aleichem sholem,*" he replied. "And unto you peace. You speak Yiddish?"

"A little. It's been a very long time."

"Come in, come in," said the old man, "warm yourself," and pointed to a small stove glowing in the corner. Peter Markovich stood before the fire and tried to thaw his frozen body.

"Have you eaten?" asked the old man. "Perhaps a little soup?"

"Thank you," said Peter Markovich.

The old man made him wash his hands and helped him recite the proper blessings, then served him a hot bowl of thick soup made from onions, potatoes, and barley. Slowly, the soup began to thaw his insides.

"I saw your menorah in the window," he said.

"Yes, this is the final night of Chanukah."

"Chanukah," repeated Peter Markovich. "My father told me to remember the Maccabees."

The old man nodded.

"Please," Peter Markovich asked, "will you recite the Chanukah blessings for me? I can't remember the words."

"Yes," said the old man, and he slowly recited the blessings. First, blessing the Holy One who sanctified us with His commandments and commanded us to kindle the Chanukah lights. Then, blessing the Holy One for performing miracles for our ancestors at this time. As Peter Markovich repeated the words with the old man, the blessings warmed his soul.

The next morning, when the commander brought soldiers to relieve Peter Markovich from his guard duty, he was surprised to find him standing at his post looking alert, strong, and confident. The blizzard had passed, and the sun was beginning to shine through the clouds, adding a bit of warmth to the air.

As Peter Markovich returned to the barracks, he tucked a small piece of wood into his knapsack. On it, faintly drawn in charcoal, was the Chanukah menorah he'd seen in the old man's window.

Peter Markovich never saw the old man again. He tried to find him. He returned to the area after his enlist- ment, but the little hut was nowhere to be found. Did the old man exist or was it all a dream? Or had the Holy One simply performed a Chanukah miracle the way he had for our ancestors so many years ago?

And so Peter Markovich, praise God, survived his years in the Tsar's army and returned to Oykvetchnik. He reunited with his family and reclaimed his name, Pinchas ben Mordechai.

The town matchmaker even found him a wife: a young widow of good character and sweet tempera- ment who was kind and optimistic, even in the face of her own hardships and difficulties. A wife who took him in and after his long journey, helped him return to his Jewishness.

Of course, it didn't take long before a child was born and then another. And every year as Chanukah arrived in Oykvetchnik, Pinchas ben Mordechai would take out the little piece of wood with the faded and smudged Chanukah menorah drawn on it. He would gather his family around him, smile at everyone with a profound joy in his heart, and tell them the story of Peter Markovich the soldier.

Seven

The Rabbi's Daughter

It was the first night of Chanukah in our little town of Oykvetchnik. An early winter snow had painted the rooftops and covered the muddy streets with a soft blanket of white, which created a scene so beautiful and serene, that even the most diehard kvetcher couldn't complain about it.

As soon as darkness fell, Chanukah lights began to appear: flickering candles behind frosted glass as Jewish families placed menorahs on windowsills in celebration of the holiday.

In the Rabbi of Oykvetchnik's home, the activities were just getting underway. Family and guests had arrived, and the Rabbi sat at the table looking around with great satisfaction.

He smiled with pleasure at the sight of his only daughter, Channele, surrounded—as usual—by a circle of boys. Channele was very beautiful—and she knew it. And although the Rabbi had tried to subdue her tendency towards vanity, he had to admit she was perfectly formed in face and figure, as if created by the Angels of heaven. Her only blemish: a tiny dark mole above her upper lip.

By the time she was of marriageable age, matchmakers from miles around were standing in line with suitors: privileged sons of rich and respected families, poor Torah scholars destined to be great rabbis, and handsome and successful businessmen seeking to improve their *yikhes*—their lineage.

Of course, the Rabbi of Oykvetchnik knew it was time for his daughter to be married. His wife, the Rebbetzin—long life to her—reminded him about it on a daily basis.

"She's not getting any younger," the Rebbetzin nudged him. "It's time for a husband and children. When I was her age—"

"Yes, yes," the Rabbi always replied, but he knew she was right.

Yet as each hopeful admirer was presented to the beautiful Channele, she turned him down on the spot. This one was too young and that one too old; this one too boring and that one too flamboyant; this one too bashful and that one too full of himself. And to be perfectly honest, the Rabbi wasn't all that disappointed. He loved his daughter dearly and wanted only the best for her. And as he surveyed the prospects he had to admit none of them were all that *ai-ai-ai.*

Now it was the Rabbi's custom on *Shabbes*—the Sabbath—to bring home a few of his students after services. He would give them a good meal, engage in a little *Shabbes* merriment, and try to brighten their lives a little.

And one of his favorite students was named Ezra ben Eliezer, truly the brightest boy in the whole yeshiva. Ezra ben Eliezer—poor thing—was an orphan. When his father died shortly after his bar mitzvah, he was sent to live with an uncle in Oykvetchnik.

This uncle immediately recognized the boy's quick mind and enrolled him in the Rabbi's yeshiva. Whether it was the fact that he was descended from a renowned rabbi—a grandfather on his mother's side—or just his innate abilities, praise God, the boy proved to be an apt and eager learner, who was very forceful in his arguments without ever offending anyone with his well-reasoned point of view.

On top of that, he was the kindest, gentlest, and most modest student the Rabbi had ever encountered. Even the Rebbetzin, with her critical eye, had to admit that Ezra ben Eliezer possessed a most special and beautiful spirit. And Channele, too, always treated Ezra ben Eliezer with the utmost courtesy.

In fact, the Rabbi couldn't recall a single time when Channele had ever acted haughty or rude to Ezra ben Eliezer—or even seemed bothered by his disfigurement.

Oy, the disfigurement. How do we talk of it? Ezra ben Eliezer was a hunchback: his twisted spine formed a hump that bent his body down and pushed his head forward, forcing him to walk as if he carried the whole burden of the Jewish Exile on his back.

And yet the boy carried this burden without resentment or anger. He simply accepted it as his fate—and the people who loved him accepted it as well.

But in truth, knowing his daughter's temperament, the Rabbi of Oykvetchnik never considered Ezra ben Eliezer a potential son-in-law—until that first night of Chanukah.

Nu, so how did this miracle happen? It happened at the table while the Rabbi's family and students—including Ezra ben Eliezer—were anxiously awaiting the arrival of the Rebbetzin's freshly fried latkes. Everyone was talking and laughing and discussing the great miracle of the oil that lasted for eight days.

Channele, who was helping her mother, came into the room with a platter filled to overflowing with latkes and began to serve the guests. And suddenly the Rabbi understood the special connection between Ezra ben Eliezer and his daughter.

What tipped him off? In all the years he had known him, the Rabbi had never seen Ezra ben Eliezer take a second look at a girl. But there on that first night of Chanukah, as Channele filled his plate with latkes, Ezra ben Eliezer looked up into her eyes. And what surprised the Rabbi even more, was that Channele returned his gaze with such humility and respect.

And suddenly the Rabbi knew that he had finally found Channele's *basherter*—her intended one, her soulmate. But how in the world was he going to convince her?

That night, the Rabbi awoke with a start. He gasped and held his heart?

"What? What is it?" asked the Rebbetzin, terrified by her husband's expression.

"Ezra ben Eliezer," whispered the Rabbi.

"What Ezra ben Eliezer?" asked the Rebbetzin.

"Ezra ben Eliezer is Channele's *basherter*."

The Rebbetzin's eyes grew wide. "What? Are you *meshugeh*? Are you crazy? Ezra ben Eliezer the hunchback?"

"Sha!" said the Rabbi. "Yes, I'm telling you: Ezra ben Eliezer."

"*Vey iz mir*," replied the Rebbetzin. "And how do you suddenly know this?"

"I had a dream."

"*Oy,* again with the dreams?"

"Listen, dear wife, I will tell you everything. Then you be the judge." And the Rabbi told the Rebbetzin his entire dream.

The next morning, the Rebbetzin sat down with Channele. "My dear daughter," she said, in a very serious tone. "As you know, it is said that forty days before we are born a voice calls out in heaven the name of our *basherter*—our intended one, the boy we are destined to stand with under the *chuppah*—the wedding canopy. But alas, once we're born, the name is forgotten."

"Oh Mama, that's just a *bobeh mayse*—an old wives' tale."

"Perhaps, my dear, but last night your father had a dream. He found himself standing in the World to Come."

"Oh Mama, not another dream. He probably just ate too many latkes."

"Hear me, daughter! As your father stood there in the World to Come, he heard a voice call out your name. And then the name of your *basherter,* your soulmate—the one chosen by heaven to be your husband.

"A boy came forward. He was handsome and straight. He possessed great intelligence, yet he was modest and gentle, and the Angels predicted he would one day become a great religious scholar and rabbi—not unlike your father.

"'We must give him a sign,' said one of the Angels, 'so he doesn't take his gifts too lightly. Something to remind him that he is not without blemish in the World Below.'

"So the Angels of heaven placed a small dark mole above his upper lip—something that would always re-mind him of life's imperfections.

"Then, my dear Channele, you were called before the Angels of heaven—such a sweet and beautiful child, graceful and charming, although your tendency to-wards vanity was apparent even then.

"All the Angels agreed that you were the perfect match for this boy, but one expressed concern: 'I fear this child's beauty may lead her to pridefulness or even arrogance, God forbid!'

"'*Oy,* what should we do?' asked the Angels. 'Per-haps another mole?'

"'No,' said the Angel, 'it must be more convincing. How about a hump on her back?'

"'A hunchback?' protested an Angel in your defense. 'That's too severe.' But the other Angels insisted.

"'Wait!' a voice spoke up. It was your intended bridegroom. 'To be a hunchback is a very difficult burden for a person to carry,' he said. 'I beg you, allow me to carry it for her. Let her be straight and beautiful—a reflection of heaven for all to see. Give her the mole and give me the hump.'

"And so the Angels, persuaded by the boy's kind words, placed your hump on his back to be carried during his lifetime here in the World Below. And you, my dear daughter, received his birthmark."

Channele touched the small mole above her upper lip and didn't need her mother to tell her the boy's name.

So Ezra ben Eliezer and Channele the Rabbi's daughter were married in Oykvetchnik. And what a magnificent celebration it was—attended by every single person in the town!

And as Channele lifted her veil to look into the loving eyes of her *basherter*—her soulmate—it was clear to everyone that this, indeed, was a marriage made in heaven.

Eight

The Pawnshop Menorah

Every year just before Chanukah, as winter pushed its way into Oykvetchnik, Reb Isaac Aronson paid a little visit to Reb Yankel's pawnshop. There, after spending a little time *kibbitzing* over a glass of tea, Reb Isaac would hand over a few coins and buy back his wife's old fur coat.

You have to understand that Reb Isaac's wife, Henye, a rather small and slender woman, was always cold, and always complaining about it: "*Oy,* I'm freezing to death," she told her family as she shivered and shook. "Doesn't anyone care if their mother turns into an icicle?"

Of course, her family cared. Who wants your mother turning into an icicle? But times were very hard, and although they had a little house, Reb Isaac was struggling to make a living. Money was scarce and Henye's old fur coat, an heirloom from her *bobie*—her grandmother—was one of the few things they owned that had any real value. That's why it spent most of the year at Reb Yankel's pawnshop.

But every winter, Reb Isaac would go and buy back Henye's coat. That way, at least between Chanukah and Purim, his dear wife had one less thing to kvetch about.

But one year, Reb Isaac not only returned from Reb Yankel's pawnshop with his wife's coat, he also had a package under his arm.

"Children, where are you? I have a present for you!"

"A present?" squealed his daughter, Rivke, a girl about twelve, as she hurried to his side.

"What is it, *Tateh?*" asked his son, Dovidl, a boy about fourteen, as he came running to look.

"Open it!" said Reb Isaac as he put the package on the table.

The children quickly untied the string and tore off the paper. What they found was an old brass menorah: dirty and tarnished and covered with cobwebs and dust.

"You bought a menorah?" asked Henye. "How can we afford a menorah at a time like this?"

"Ah, Henye, don't worry," said Reb Isaac. "It didn't cost us a kopeck. Reb Yankel gave it to me for the children. He said he has to make room for all the new merchandise poor people will be bringing him during the winter months.

"He said this old menorah has been sitting on a shelf gathering dust for years, but nobody ever came back to claim it. He said it was time to give it a new home."

"*Tateh*, it's beautiful!" said Dovidl.

Rivke made a face. "Beautiful? It's filthy!"

"But we can clean it up!" said Dovidl.

"Clean it up? It'll take us forever!"

"Children," said Reb Isaac, "what if we put our new menorah in Dovidl's care?"

"Really, *Tateh?*"

"Yes, Dovidl. Let's see what you can do with it?"

So that afternoon, Dovidl scrubbed and rubbed and cleaned that old menorah. He dried it, polished it, and buffed it.

And when he was done—except for a small crack in one of the branches—the menorah sparkled as if it were brand new. Dovidl called everyone over to see it.

"Is that the same menorah?" asked Rivke.

"Good job, Dovidl!" said Reb Isaac, patting him on the shoulder.

And even his mother, after kvetching a little about the mess he had made, smiled and said, "How beautiful!"

That evening, just before supper, as the family prepared to recite the Chanukah blessings, Reb Isaac gave Dovidl the honor of lighting the first candle.

"Really, *Tateh?*"

"Yes, Dovidl, you've earned it!"

The whole family gathered around their beautiful new menorah as Dovidl proudly lit the first candle. Then Reb Isaac placed the menorah on the windowsill, and everyone sat down to enjoy Henye's delicious latkes.

And that's when it happened—

"*Tateh,*" screamed Rivke.

"What is it, Rivke?"

"In the window—there's a face in the window!"

Everyone ran over to look, and there in the window, pressing his face against the glass, was Zalman the Beggar.

"It's Zalman!" said Henye.

"*Tateh,* what's he doing out there?" asked Dovidl.

"Sha," said Reb Isaac as he opened the door. "Reb Zalman, why are you standing outside on such a cold night? Come in, warm yourself."

"Mama, he's inviting him in!"

"Hush, Rivke."

"Oh, I couldn't, Reb Isaac," mumbled Reb Zalman.

"You must, Reb Zalman, it's freezing out here. Come in, come in and have latkes with us."

"Oh, no!"

"Please, Reb Zalman. It's Chanukah."

And so very reluctantly into the little house came Reb Zalman, the town beggar. Reb Isaac took him to wash his hands, and Henye set a place for him at the table between Rivke and Dovidl.

"He smells bad, Mama!"

"Quiet, Rivke!"

But Rivke was right. Reb Zalman smelled awful. He was an old man, and he spent most of his time on the streets begging for money. His coat was tattered and patched, and his beard was gray and straggly.

Everyone knew Reb Zalman the Beggar. People said that his children had deserted him, and now, too old and frail to work, he wandered the streets begging for food and money.

When Reb Zalman was finally seated at the table, Henye brought out the first plate of latkes. And suddenly, everyone forgot all about how bad Reb Zalman smelled. One taste of Henye's latkes and everything else was forgotten. Chanukah became a real celebration!

When the feast was over, and everyone was sitting back in their chairs full and happy, Reb Zalman cleared his throat. "I cannot tell you how grateful I am to you Reb Isaac—to you and your family. It has been many years—almost a lifetime—since I have eaten such a good meal and tasted such delicious latkes. I remember many years ago when *my* family celebrated Chanukah with latkes and the lighting of candles. We, too, had a beautiful menorah, just like the one in your window.

"That is why I stopped tonight. My eyesight is not so good anymore, and I had to take a closer look—it reminded me so much of the menorah we used to own."

"What happened to it, Reb Zalman?" asked Rivke.

"Times were very difficult for my family. First, I lost my job—may it never happen to you. Then my beloved wife—rest in peace—left this world for the World to Come. So before another misfortune could befall my family—God forbid—I made a decision to send my children away to America where they could make a better life for themselves. So I took everything we owned to the pawnshop for money. All our valuable possessions—including our beautiful menorah."

"Was it Reb Yankel's pawnshop?" Dovidl asked.

"Oh, it was such a long time ago, I don't remember. What I do remember is how beautiful it looked on the windowsill, polished and gleaming, candles burning brightly. And I remember, too, a little crack in one of the branches—we always had to be so careful when we put in all the candles."

And that's when Dovidl knew he had Reb Zalman's menorah!

"That spring," Reb Zalman continued, "I bought tickets on a steamer ship for my son and his wife, and for my two daughters, and sent them off to live with my older brother and his family in America. They said that someday they would send for me, and—God willing— someday they will. At least that is my dream."

"God willing, Reb Zalman," said Henye gently. "God willing."

Slowly Reb Zalman stood up from the table. "I must go now and leave you in peace. Thank you, Reb Isaac, for inviting me to be your guest. You have warmed my body and my soul. A blessing on you and your family."

As Reb Zalman was leaving, Dovidl thought to himself, "Should I tell him we have his menorah?" But then he thought, "What would he do with it? Probably just pawn it again. And I've worked so hard to make it beautiful!"

At the door, Henye handed Reb Zalman a little package filled with latkes, and Reb Isaac slipped him a few coins.

"Thank you for your kindness," said Reb Zalman. "Good night to you and your family. And happy Chanukah to you all."

"Wait, Reb Zalman!" Dovidl suddenly called out. "You can't leave yet!"

"Why not?"

"Reb Zalman, I have something to tell you: We have your menorah."

"My menorah?"

"Yes! *Tateh* brought it home from the pawnshop. It has a little crack in one of the branches, just like you said! You must take it with you, Reb Zalman."

"Take it with me? Oh, my dear young man, if it is indeed our beloved menorah, then I am so grateful it has found such a wonderful new home with someone who loves it as much as I do and is willing to take such good care of it.

"Keep it safe, young man. Treasure it always. It is a symbol of our freedom. And perhaps someday you will let me come visit it again."

"Yes, Reb Zalman, yes!" said Dovidl.

That was the last time they saw Reb Zalman the Beggar. That spring Reb Zalman's dream came true: he received a ticket to America from his family.

But that's not where the story ends.

A few months later, as Reb Isaac's ability to earn a living became even more difficult, and as the political climate in Oykvetchnik became more violent towards the Jews, the family decided that they, too, should sell all their belongings and sail to America—"The land of milk and honey; of hope and opportunity."

As they prepared to leave, Reb Isaac ordered everyone to take only what they could pack in their suitcases. "If it doesn't fit in your suitcase," he said, "you must leave it behind."

On the day of their departure, Reb Isaac lined everyone up to check what they had packed. That's when he discovered Reb Zalman's menorah in Dovidl's suitcase.

"Dovidl—" said Reb Isaac.

"Yes, *Tateh?*"

"Dovidl—it will look good on our windowsill in America."

And that, my friends, is how Reb Zalman's menorah made it to America.

Happy Chanukah!

ACKNOWLEDGMENTS

First and foremost, I must thank Maxine Carr and the members of the Raleigh-Cary Jewish Community Center's Speaker Luncheon group for allowing me to share and polish these stories with them over the past several years. Their enthusiastic and loving responses have encouraged the writing of these Chanukah tales.

I am indebted to my parents, Bernard Morris and Doris Davis of blessed memory, and my teachers Sabell Bender and Ethel Weinstein for firmly planting in my heart the seeds of Jewish music, literature, drama, and culture. Throughout my lifetime, they have nurtured and encouraged my interest in performing Jewish stories and writing my own tales.

"The Rabbi's Daughter" was inspired by a Jewish folktale, "Made In Heaven," which I found in Hava Ben-Zvi's wonderful collection, *The Bride Who Argued*

with God: Tales From the Treasury of Jewish Folklore.
Over the years, Mrs. Ben-Zvi has become a cherished friend, and I am thankful for her permission to adapt the tale for this book.

Sincerest thanks to the following people who assisted in refining and proofreading the manuscript: Curt Leviant, Arthur Clark, Lynn Padgett, Judith Pine Bobé, Kathleen Southern, and Michael Bassman.

Deepest appreciation to my sister, Robin Evans, who has been a faithful advisor and editor, and to her husband, Jim, for his patience and good-humored insights.

Finally, I am grateful to Carolyn Toben for her unending support, encouragement, and love.

GLOSSARY

Ai-ai-ai. A happy, sad, or disdainful exclamation depending on the circumstances.

Alteh. Old.

Bar mitzvah. The initiation ceremony conducted when a boy turns thirteen and assumes the responsibilities and privileges of an adult in the Jewish community.

Basherter. A woman's intended one or soulmate. A man's intended one is called his *besherteh.*

Bobeh. Grandmother.

Bobeh mayse. Grandmother's tale or old wives' tale.

Bobie. Grandmother.

Chanukiyah. The nine-branched Chanukah menorah.

Chuppah. Wedding canopy.

Dreidel. A small four-sided top used in a gambling game during Chanukah.

Gonif. Thief.

Guteh neshomeh. A good soul.

Hora. A lively circle dance with roots in Eastern European folk tradition.

Kabbalah. Jewish mysticism.

Kibbitzing. Chatting.

Kiddish cup. Ceremonial cup used during the benediction over wine.

Klezmer. Jewish musicians and the style of music they play.

Kosher. Food prepared according to Jewish law.

Kvetch. Complain.

Latkes. Potato pancakes fried in oil.

Mazel. Luck.

Menorah. The traditional seven-branched candelabra used in the synagogue. Also used to refer to the nine-branched candelabra used during Chanukah.

Mentsh. A person; a moral and ethical person of worth and integrity.

Meshugeh, meshugeneh. Crazy.

Mezuzah. A box or case that contains a small parchment scroll with two blessings from the Torah. The mezuzah is fastened to the doorpost of a house or building.

Mitzvah. Good deed; commandment.

Myzeleh. Little mouse.

Nosh. To eat or munch on something.

Nu. An interjection similar to the words "so?" "so what?" or "well."

Oy. Similar to the expression, "Oh my!"

Oy gevalt. Similar to the expression, "Oh trouble!"

Oy vey. Similar to the expression, "Oh no!"

Rabbi. Jewish religious leader and teacher.

Reb. A title of respect similar to "Sir" or "Mister."

Rebbetzin. Rabbi's wife.

Schlemiel. An inept or foolish person.

Schlimazel. An unlucky person.

Shabbes. The Sabbath.

Shammes. Caretaker of a synagogue; the candle used to light the other Chanukah candles.

Sholem aleichem. An expression of greeting that means "peace unto you." The response in return is *aleichem sholem,* "and unto you peace."

Shtetl. Small Jewish town or village in Russia and Eastern Europe.

Shul. Synagogue.

Tateh. Father.

Torah. The holy scroll on which the five books of Moses is written.

Tzedakah. Charity.

Vey iz mir. Similar to the expression, "Woe is me."

Yarmulke. Skull cap.

Yeshiva. A Jewish institution of religious learning.

Yikhes. Lineage.

Yorzeit. The anniversary of a death.

Zay gezunt. Be well.

Zaydeh. Grandfather.

About the Author

 Scott Hilton Davis is a lifelong storyteller, filmmaker, author, and collector of Jewish short stories written in the late nineteenth and early twentieth centuries.

Scott began his acting career as a child performing in Jewish skits and plays in Los Angeles, California, and now offers his stories and talks to synagogues, Jewish Community Centers, cultural clubs, and religious school audiences across the country.

Convinced of the historical, cultural, and ethical significance of stories by Sholem Aleichem, I. L. Peretz, Sholem Abramovitsh, and Jacob Dinezon, Scott began using storytelling to bring the works of these beloved Jewish writers to new audiences. As part of this effort, he published the first English translation of Jacob Dinezon's autobiographical short stories, *Memories and Scenes: Shtetl, Childhood, Writers.*

Scott is the author of *Souls Are Flying! A Celebration of Jewish Stories* and has produced and directed Emmy Award-winning documentaries and dramas for public television. He lives in Raleigh, North Carolina.

Souls Are Flying!
A Celebration of Jewish Stories

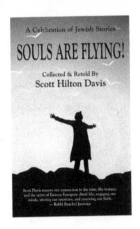

Late in the nineteenth century, an explosion of Jewish creativity produced an outpouring of inspiring short stories to help readers cope with the turbulent effects of modernity on traditional Jewish life in Eastern Europe. In this collection of twelve retold tales, storyteller Scott Hilton Davis offers humorous, poignant, and powerful examples by four of the most beloved Jewish writers of this period: Sholem Aleichem, I. L. Peretz, Sholem Abramovitsh (considered the classic writers of modern Yiddish literature), and their colleague and friend, Jacob Dinezon.

Featured in this revised edition of *Souls Are Flying!* are characters such as the Old Book Peddler who struggles to travel his own path; the poor *Melamud* (a Hebrew school teacher of young children) who imagines the world he would create if he were the wealthy banker Rothschild; the orphan boy who learns how to be a *mentsh* (an honorable person); and the *Litvak,* a skeptic from Lithuania, who discovers the heavenly power of a simple good deed.

Although written more than a hundred years ago, these retold tales with their quintessential Jewish values hold important insights for people of all faiths who struggle with today's issues of social injustice, poverty, violence, war, and the challenge of living a life of integrity in a world that seems constantly in turmoil.

MEMORIES AND SCENES
SHTETL, CHILDHOOD, WRITERS

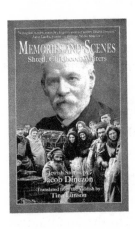

"Jacob Dinezon's newly translated masterpiece belongs next to Sholem Aleichem's works."
—*Jewish Daily Forward*

"With Dinezon's *Memories and Scenes,* we happily encounter a master writer who deserves to be ranked with Sholom Aleichem and I. L. Peretz."
—*Hadassah Magazine*

"Highly recommended."
—*Association of Jewish Libraries Reviews*

In August of 2014, the English-speaking world received access to a short-story collection by the once-beloved author Jacob Dinezon, a central figure in the development of Yiddish as a literary language at the turn of the twentieth century.

This profound and delightful collection, translated from the Yiddish by Tina Lunson, paints a vivid portrait of life in the small shtetl towns of Eastern Europe. Amid poverty and strict adherence to Jewish law and customs, Dinezon's characters struggle to reconcile their heartfelt impulses with strict religious teachings and social norms.

In *Memories and Scenes: Shtetl, Childhood, Writers*, a humble tailor finds, in an old whiskey flask, the courage to speak out against poverty and inequality. The life of an orphan boy is thrown into turmoil by the relentless pressure of a matchmaker. An old Torah teacher, shunned by the community for his interest in modern mathematics, comes to understand the poetic beauty of nature from his artistic student. And an entire town is thrown into chaos by the antics of a sacred community goat.

Dinezon's poignant and provocative characters paint a vivid portrait of late nineteenth century Eastern European shtetl life and provide readers with a treasure trove of Jewish history, culture, and values.

HERSHELE
A JEWISH LOVE STORY

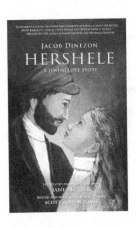

"A gripping tale with a realistic adolescent love story,
a complicated plot, and an unexpected ending."
—*Association of Jewish Libraries Reviews*

"A sweet, ageless romance that has
stood the test of time."
—*Foreword Reviews*

In 1891, the Yiddish writer Jacob Dinezon crafted
a tender love story exploring the budding romance between two young people separated by class and tradition.
This compelling fable, created with equal measures of
hope and despair, charmed his many readers, but until
recently has remained inaccessible to modern audiences.

Hershele is the bittersweet love story of Hershele and Mirele—he a penniless yeshiva student with no family, she the lovely daughter of a widow who provides a weekly charity meal to poor students. Their unlikely meeting generates a strong attraction that gradually overcomes the powerful obstacles of social norms and class status. But determined forces are arrayed against them, and their first tentative steps toward modernity are challenged at every turn.

Hershele, translated from the Yiddish by Jane Peppler, is at once a fascinating glimpse into the daily life of Eastern European Jews in the late nineteenth century, and the extremely personal and poignant story of two young lovers trapped in the realities of the clash between existing traditions and social change. It is simultaneously a historical novel and a timeless tale of romance. In its own way, *Hershele* is the Romeo and Juliet story of the shtetl.

Yosele

A Story from Jewish Life

A story so poignant and powerful it transformed the Jewish educational system of Eastern Europe.

In 1899, Jacob Dinezon's short novel, *Yosele,* exposed in vivid detail the outmoded and cruel teaching methods prevalent in the traditional cheders (Jewish elementary schools) of the late 1800s.

Writing in Yiddish to reach the broadest Jewish audience, Dinezon described the sad, poverty-stricken, and violent life of a bright and gentle schoolboy whose treatment at the hands of his teacher, parents, and rich society is heartrending, painful, and shocking.

The pathos and outrage resulting from the story's initial publication produced an urgent call for reform and set the stage for the establishment of a secular school movement that transformed Jewish elementary education in the early 1900s.

Translated into English for the first time by Jane Peppler, Jacob Dinezon's *Yosele* presents a rarely seen sociological and cultural picture of Eastern European Jewish life at the end of the nineteenth century.

Jacob Dinezon
The Mother Among
Our Classic Yiddish Writers

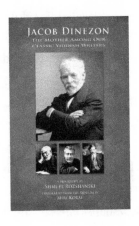

Was there a fourth classic Yiddish writer? This is what the renowned literary historian Shmuel Rozshanski asserts in this insightful and well-documented biography about the beloved and successful nineteenth century Yiddish author, Jacob Dinezon (1851?-1919), called by the *Jewish Daily Forward*, "The Greatest Yiddish Writer You Never Heard Of."

Credited with writing the first "Jewish Realistic Romance" and the first bestselling Yiddish novel, Dinezon was closely associated with the leading Jewish writers of his day, including Sholem Abramovitsh (Mendele Mocher Sforim), Sholem Aleichem, and I. L. Peretz—

dubbed the "Classic Writers of Modern Yiddish Literature."

Dinezon wrote poignant stories about Eastern European shtetl life and focused on the emotional conflicts affecting young people as modern ideas challenged traditional religious practices and social norms. He was also a staunch advocate of Yiddish as a literary language, and a highly respected community philanthropist.

In this extensively researched Yiddish biography written in 1956 and translated into English by Yiddishist Miri Koral, Shmuel Rozshanski makes the case for including Jacob Dinezon in the "family" of classic Yiddish writers. If, as scholars suggest, Sholem Abramovitsh is the grandfather, I. L. Peretz the father, and Sholem Aleichem the grandson of modern Yiddish literature, then Jacob Dinezon, Rozshanski insists, should be considered the "mother" for his gentle, kindhearted, and emotional approach to storytelling and his readers.

An important new research book for scholars of Yiddish literature, history, and culture.

To learn more about these books
and others, please visit

JEWISH STORYTELLER PRESS
www.jewishstorytellerpress.com

CPSIA information can be obtained
at www.ICGtesting.com
Printed in the USA
LVHW092334191121
703740LV00021B/540